GET INTIMATE

By

Nikeema T. Lee

This book is a beginning.
Spanning 17 years. It is
written from the prospective
of an undereducated teenager.
You will find misspelled
words and lack of proper
grammar use. Please read
with an open mind and an
open heart.

1

November 21, 1977

Today started off like any other day. We all rose early to meet at the gathering table to break bread, speak of our dreams had the night before to the elders' and work in the Garden of Promise. This was our way of life. This was a place where we found honor and joy. Breaking of bread was the opportunity for us to give thanks to our Father for providing us with our daily nourishment. Speaking of our <u>Dreams</u> was always a festive event in the morning. It allowed for the family to usher in understanding and wisdom of our Father's Love. Many members of my family frequently had reoccurring episodes of revelation and I was no different. For as far back as I could remember, my dreams would consist of me playing in the Garden of Promise with my Father, so it was to my surprise that on the previous night I had encountered a completely different dream. As I awoke I quickly dressed, ate and anticipated my turn to tell the elders of my new story.

As I waited for my opportunity to share, my stomach turned and churned, twisted and pulled. I have never felt such a feeling in the pit of my soul. I felt as if the revelation from this dream would change my life without even knowing what it meant. Slowly, we went around in the circle and my moment finally approached. So built up with joy and the unknown I blurted out with a raised voice, "I had a new dream last night." The room fell silent. You could hear the flow of the water transgressing through fountains and the songs of the birds come together to sing one unifying note, as if time had stood still just to hear of my new dream. "Well my young child, do tell us of your new revelation." "There was a house immaculately placed, I started, on a cliff surrounded by sand that overlooked a beach." They all stared as if there was more. "Is that all my child," asked the elder? With all the excitement of having a new dream that was all I could remember, "Yes". After only a few moments of conversing with the others, the elder of the family told me that to see the beach in my dream, symbolizes the meeting between my two states of mind.

The sand is symbolic of the rational and mental processes while the water signifies the irrational, unsteady, and emotional aspects of ones self. It is a place of transition between the physical/material and the spiritual. To dream that you are standing at the edge of a cliff indicates that you have arrived to an increased level of understanding, new awareness, and a fresh point of view. You may have reached a critical point in your life and may face the fear of losing control. "My child, today you shall not be afraid. Let your soul rewrite your destiny and let faith keep you whole. Your Father has given you this revelation; honor it by preparing your heart to receive the call".

Having all shared our dreams; it was time to begin our

days work in the Garden of Promise. The Garden of Promise brought us all such joy. Everywhere you looked you could see the fruits of your labor. Bright hues of reds, purples, yellow, oranges and greens---mixed and mingled with each other. Tulips, Irises, Daffodils and Gladioli as far as the eye could see---sang together with a soft harmony. To be in the Garden was a promise that we all had made to our Father, when we were old enough to understand the teachings of his Love.

Now Father was a gentle and loving spirit. He had a glow around HIM that could blind you. Our world was filled with so many hearts that loved and adored HIM. Everyday it seems like thousands upon thousands would flock to the steps of his lighthouse just to see him. My sister told me that Father once showered the hearts of a crowd so heavily that their hearts filled and began to over flow, spilling their love onto the ground below, that's why the place in the Garden where only the roses grow is called "Love Over Flowing" Lane. To me, Father is the greatest gift to my life. I never have to ask for anything, you know, it's like he could read my soul and know my needs. Father is known for not just HIS love but also of HIS compassion for HIS children. He watches over us from HIS lighthouse window.

Father did all HIS work in the lighthouse. Anytime day or night, Father was at the Lighthouse. The Lighthouse was this warm and inviting place that just drew itself to you. It had a smooth black surface that appeared seamless and large shiny windows that wrapped around the Lighthouse as if it was a portal to a new world. On the top were these radiant lights that always illuminated the sky.

The lights had the same colors of that which could be found within the Garden. In the day's sun, it looked like the hues of the Garden reflected onto the lighthouse, creating such a wonderful glow. Sometimes during the day I would find myself just daydreaming and in amazement of the Lighthouse and thinking about when Father will make HIS daily announcement to HIS children.

You see, everyday, Father would call down from the Lighthouse to one of us. The call was always a surprise; for none of us knew the time in which the call would come. One the first day of entry into the Garden you were told that one day, Father would call upon one of HIS children to do a very special project. This project was so special that Father only chose his most beloved child.

The Garden Keeper also told us that this calling would come everyday and that we should always be prepared for it. I remember one of my brothers with me the day I came to the Garden, asked the Garden Keeper, "Will I know if I'm ready or even prepared?" The Garden Keeper responded with such tenderness, "if you are here, you are ready and the Garden will prepare you." So everyday the call from my Father would create such an overwhelming amount of excitement and praise from his children. We all knew that this was our destiny. The sacrifice of leaving our brothers and sisters to go and serve Father in HIS special project was a true delight. To give all we were and all we had in order to fulfill HIS purpose....man, words can not even articulate the emotion that resonate deep within the bowels of ones soul.

Whenever someone would come back from special project work, they would converse on and on about how

Father saved them and protected them. Father would bestow, upon those who returned, treasures of the land by way of Lighthouses in the Golden Dandelion Garden. This location of the Garden was made especially for the returnees. Golden Dandelion Garden was a gated spot of the Garden that none of us had ever seen, but the story is told that the streets are lined with Golden Dandelions and that water flowed out of the rocks. They say that Father built it HIMSELF for the first returnee as a thank you for all his work in bringing back Fathers lost children. They also say that Father is planning on letting him go back someday to rescue more lost children in time for the great celebration.

So today when the horns sounded and Father Came to the front door, it felt like the door took so long to open. Suddenly the revelation of my dreams started to re-emerge vividly within my mind as if I was having it all over again. I could hear the voice of the elder say, "trust your heart and face your fears." As the door slowly opened, my eyes began to water and I felt this slow rising in my stomach. More and more the door creped ajar as my stomach match with intensity and suddenly….the rising inside of me busted forward and I leapt toward my Father.

Leaping over the bright hues of reds, purples, yellows, oranges and greens, I sprang like the animals in the gathering fields. Over Tulips, Irises, Daffodils and Gladioli as far as the eye could see. My brothers and sisters were praising, shouting and crying as I ascended passed them, on a one way encounter with my Father. My mind unaware my body was moving, I gazed at the eyes of my Father and warmth passed through me in such an overwhelming rush of comfort that I reached for HIM. Longing to finally fulfill a promise made, wanting to complete the balance of an ever wanted embrace. My Father has called me and I shall go.

"It's your time my child"! Tears began to pour from my eyes as for all my dreams were to come true all at that moment. I had been chosen and I knew that I was ready. It was my time to show Father that I could do it and that it could be done by me. Finally I was in the arms of Father and in the Lighthouse. I was in the Lighthouse!

Inside the Lighthouse were these huge pillars of stone

that rose and rose until you would lose sight of them. I tried to look around but I was blinded by tears. My heart was pounding----leaping out of my body and my mouth became dry and tasteless. I couldn't breath. I felt dizzy and weak. I began to tremble and suddenly I let out a blessed sound, "AH" and again "AH" and louder "AH". "Yes, my child, let go of your way and embrace MY way, as you speak my name. For now you have entered into my presence and I shall bless you. Your work in the Garden of Promise has prepared you for my special project".

As I wept I began to look into Father's eye and oh---- how he touched my soul. The love that poured out of his eyes, encapsulated my heart rendering me submissive. I began to bow at his feet and just wept. It was such an honor to have been chosen. Father raised me up and we began to walk toward a big book lit in the center of the room. "This book holds the names of all MY children who have been chosen to perform special projects for me and I shall write you name amongst my beloved.

Never forget that you are my chosen child sent to fulfill

a promise and to being about a new according to divine direction." "Oh Father I will never forget what has happened here for I will always know in my heart that you are my Father and that in YOU is to whom I owe my life."

We began to walk toward a big door with golden trim. The door had this big lion's head in the middle but it had no handles. "My child, everything you've learned in the Garden of Promise will be required to succeed. Know that I love you and I will always be at your side." The big red door opens and before me is an endless room of black. The air within is still, calm just like the air within in the Garden. Father turned to me and says, "I need you to speak to the people and remind them of my love. Your journey must be filled with lows in order to speak truthfully of the heights in which I must take you.

Do not be troubled by life for I will never burden your soul with more then you can stand. Speak of my love. I will never leave you to be alone in your thoughts but I will forever live in your heart. Trust in yourself and you shall find refuge in me. I love you. You were created just for this task. You love for me shall only grow stronger as your life's journey grows longer. Love yourself as you would love me and I will never be far from you. This is your destiny."

I now have my assignment. I must do all I can to complete my mission. I can not let Father down. So with all that power at by back, I take a deep breath and take my first step into the darkness. I know that I must continue to walk this path that Father has prepared for me. Father kisses me with the sweetest of kisses and tells me that if ever I need him to just call his name and he will be there.

The door closes and the darkness becomes complete, there is no turning back now. I turn and walk. I walk and walk…and walk and walk. I began on my journey one step at a time---I walk. To make sure I would not forget my destiny I keep repeating it in my mind over and over again: speak to the people and remind them of my love. It seemed as if I wasn't even moving. The darkness was endless; it traveled all together, all around, all encompassing---endless. The darkness began to take my mind and I grew tired. I figure I should rest, just for a moment. I'll just lie down…then I heard a voice. "What am I going to do? What do you want me to do? I could give a damn about you and that damn baby. What! Fuck you motherfucker."

I was startled with all the yelling. I call out to find who's out there, "Hello, Hello" No one answers my calls. The yelling continues as if two people were in disagreement with life and I was caught in the middle. My ears as well as my heart began to ache. Covering my ears to drown out the noise was to no avail. The female voice was a child of Father's because she would call out to him after the male voice would stop talking. She cried and asked Father to help her.

The feeling that I felt, I had never felt before but it was heavy and cold. I yell back to her, "Don't worry, Father will help you. You are where you need to be in your journey. She was hurting so bad that I would fell her pain and have to cry out for Father to help me. Father came and kissed me and say, "Hold on my child your true journey shall begin soon. Hold on and know that I am with you always."

The no since of time in this darkness, it was only when Father came that I had a clear vision on where I was. As my days grew longer I and I grew more tried of my existence, I remember the day the flood water came. The water rushed in so quickly, completely taking me by surprise. Father appeared has if he was walking on it when he told me that it was time to go and start on my long journey to fulfilling HIS purpose.

He said at the end of the tunnel you will not remember me until due time but rest a sure that you will not forget me. I am in your heart and I will reemerge in due season. I love you, now go. SO I walked slowly to the tunnel with out any fear. I passed through the tunnel I began to fell cold and wet. My eyes fused shut and my mind clear of all things as if they were lock away from me. I could hear the tinker of what sounded like tools in the distance. I continue to try and open my eyes. Finally they opened and I saw this shadow that looked like Father.

Father I said but nothing came out but cries. Father I made it, is that you, I made it. Father said nothing to me as if I had said nothing. I made it Father I made it. Suddenly a strange voice unfamiliar to me spoke over my life and said, "IT'S A GIRL"

2

1985: Tranquil Waters

Hey my name is Mecca Janae Daniels and looking at the sea of faces I can't help but to become sick to my stomach. They... who are they anyway? Some sort of self appointing governing body that has chosen to dictate their opinion on the lives of everyone else. Fuck them! But I digress... anyway THEY always say, that to graduate from high school was a pinnacle point in a young person's life and is usually met with an overwhelming feeling of freedom followed by the desire to relive it all over again.

The feeling that raced over me was one of repulse, followed quickly by the joy of that <u>Dream</u> they refer to as freedom. The latter of that statement was truly never uttered with me in mind. I, for one, don't even want to relive the nightmare experienced at High School not to mention in the city of dream killers. Now don't get me wrong, not all my time spent in the streets were bad, I had some good times but during the course of my adventures I was hallowed out and left for dead. Left to fill my shell with… well lets just say that one man's trash was something that I treasured.

I've always contemplated this very moment, this space in time, which I was to be freed from the oppression of being an unwanted soul in a world of endless possibilities. Day after day I would visualize just walking away from all this and actually reclaim myself back from the people holding my essence for ransom. Taunting me with an impending reunion, only to raise the stakes beyond my reach once the initial bargain had been struck. Each time, they demand more and returning less. Now I know what you're thinking...in four years, your life was stolen and put up for auction like a traveler of the middle passage. No, high school was just a backdrop for a story that had started many years before I even knew my essence was in a hostage situation.

My story starts back about ten years ago, summer of 1985 to be exact. The city where this story initiates is really like any other city in America. It had all the signs of the city that it was to become. Many other cities around the country displayed the same characteristics of a place once held high for its riches, infiltrated by the lower class and left for dead by its now wealthier inhabitants in order to seek bigger and better while systematically leaving behind a distinctive group of people. This was my city. Now at seven, I really did notice the slow transgression from one level to the next, and really by the start of 1985 you really did notice much. My childhood was spent running and playing on the street of my city. Up until this time, being me was relatively carefree. I didn't remember life being no more then a summer vacation... all the time. The summer of 1985 was shaping up to be a rather unique moment. In what seemed like an overnight phenomenon. Right out of nowhere, the city went from a child's retreat to a callous operating evil.

My city was actually one of the nation's planned industrial cities. Praised for its Great Falls and ability to provide hydroelectric power, it welcomed all races and ethical backgrounds. My city thrived in the textile industry, a once leader in the game. I can remember being in love with this city that called me daughter and whom I'd called friend. For the first time I experienced something from my city that I would have the misfortune to experience time and time again------- betrayal. A city once rich in silken fabrics and people, turned into an all too common walking nightmare. A monster in the shape of a little white rock infiltrated our cities borders and set up camp in our homes. Spreading its poison like a plague far worse then anything the world had ever seen, rapidly destroying anything in its path. 1985, Crack Cocaine came on the scene and turned my beautiful city into an Eastern European war zone. Drugs weren't new to the city. We had Dope, Coke, and Weed but Crack was different. Crack pitted brother against brother and neighbor against neighbor but worst of all it pitted mother against child.

In my community fathers were few and far between so many of us were raised by single mothers and devoted grandmas. Crack killed the love that a mother had for a child and replaced it with an opportunity to escape from life. We children were no match. We couldn't compete with a ride that took you away from the hardships of an unforgiving nation. A nation that didn't consider you worth saving, that constantly reminded you of your inferior standings in this world. A nation that was counting down the days until your impending self destruction... Tick...Tock...Tick...Tock.

We pushed on the worn shoulders of women that had held the lives of so many before them, demanding that they give of themselves not knowing that what we demanded did not exist. We were poor adversaries for a full ride to mental freedom; escapism in all its glory. We were no competition for that type of joy. Our mother's were lost to this high and as abandoned children we were forced to face the lows of life on our own.

Ten years ago in 1985, I was seven and life for me seemed so innocent. I had the craziest but most loving family. My mom's side of the family was defiantly the craziest, but no matter how much they would fight or fuss you always knew that they loved you. I had aunts and uncles that were the Kings and Queens of the streets. They ran the neighborhood from the schools to the local hangouts, my people were legendary.

My cousins and I were paraded around town like Princes' and for me the only Princess, that title given to me with full pomp and circumstance. I relished in my role. I was smart and beautiful and a day did not go by that I wasn't reminded of that wonderful fact. I could do no wrong and I knew it. I was what some may say a spoiled child but I wasn't, I knew better then that.

For seven years I had the best life. The best part about that time is that everybody was well... mentally, physically, and emotionally... well. Even though my mom and her brothers and sisters had lost their mother many years before I was born, they had each other. The love they had for family was so strong. We were a true ride or die family. Nobody messed with us and everybody knew not to try. After my grandmother was killed in a car accident her two older daughters took control of the family. They did everything possible to keep the family together. Both of them post high school educated, encourage all the others to seek refuge in education, demanding that they each work hard and study harder. To their success all six of the children graduated high school, it's after that where life takes a different turn of them all.

I have always wondered if my grandmother were alive today what she would have to say about her children. Three of her eight children are with her in heaven and the other five are down here raising hell. Cursed to bear the plague of addiction, they have all fell victims to the monster that invaded our city walls. Crack took a personal interest in our family as if it had been created just for us, reducing strong minded and talented warriors to mindless zombies that wandered the street awaiting their next fix.

I watch my aunts and uncles slowly betray their family values for the love of this poison. Time after time falling deeper and deeper into a coma of death, striving for the possibility of having that moment like the first time. It was tough to watch hopes and dreams of so many smoked, snorted and injected away as if they were never dreamt. My mom seemed to be immune from this plague. She carried a job and moved us into a better neighborhood. I never saw any signs or symptoms that she too was infected.

My mom was beautiful. Even back then she could stop traffic just by her smile. Now granted she had false teeth but she had a Fem Fetal quality about her. I never saw her without make up, her hair flawless and she never went out of the house without her famous Lee Press-On Nails. Of the family, she was defiantly the rock star with the true Diva potential and she kept a flock of groupies.

Men catered to my mother's every want and need and were often subjected to her cruel treatment that stripped them of any dignity and questioned any manhood that was left to endure the suffrage. Men to my mom where a dime a dozen and in order to get with her, you better make sure you had plenty of dimes.

My mom was always involved with guys that had money so I always would reap the benefits of her having those relationships. My mom would always dress me in the finest of clothes and I always had my hair just as flawless. Many of the kids in the projects that I grew up in would always be jealous of me so talking tough was something that I became proficient in.

At seven I had everything any kid would have loved to have clothes, toys…money. Can you imagine what impact that has on seven years old? I learned early that fairly tails are nothing but fantasy and that reality is tougher then anyone wants to admit. I also learned that summer that gifts come with a price. Who could have known that payment for all the gifts that had ever been given would cost so much.

Such a high price to pay! A payment that left me bankrupt even before I was qualified to request a loan. Can you picture an emotional bank in debt long before the first real deposit was ever made.

Popsicles

I still smell his skin today. My mom went somewhere, maybe to the laundry or something but it seemed like she had been gone for a really long time. I really didn't think much of it that day; it was really just like any other day. She would often leave me alone with people while she would go out with her boyfriends. I was pretty use to being by myself.

On this particular day I really didn't think that anything would be any different. I was lying on my bed in our one bedroom apartment. For projects standards these were some of the better ones in the city. They actually had a play area with a slide and monkey bars. It was only two buildings and six floors so there weren't too many people living in one place. To add to the fact that these projects were somewhat set outside of the city, you could get the sense of being in a different town.

Our neighborhood was safe enough to leave your children home alone, so I felt OK being there. That day I wasn't home alone I had company.

When guys would stay at the house I generally would just hang out in the room and wait until my mother would come home.

"Hey, have you seen where your mommy put my shoes?" He said.

"I think she put it in the closet."

Now because my bed was directly in front of the closet I had to get up in order to let him get in.

"Hey, what are you doing?" He asked.

"Nothing"

He paused "You know that one day I'm going to marry your mother and then you will be my daughter. Would you like to be my daughter? I promise I will take care of you and your mother".

"Yeah, I said. I would like that. I like you. I think that you're a nice guy".

"Well, he said as he reached into the closet, I like you too. I really love your mommy. Do you think that you will love me the same way that your mommy loves me?"

"I guess"

"Do you think that I can get a hug like your mommy gives to me?"

"Sure" I said. So I hugged him because he was a good guy that promised to love me and my mommy and he would always give us stuff. One Christmas he gave me a microwave and a color TV. Whenever he came over he would bring gifts and always had money rolled up with rubber bands. His hug got a little tight so I started to let him go.

"Don't let me go! I like your hugs. They feel real nice. Do you give anybody else hugs like that?"

"No" I said.

"Well you better not. I can't have my daughter going around giving give out hugs that are only meant for me. Do you know what goes good with hugging?"

"No. What?"

"Kissing" he said with a smile place on his face. I really thought that he was just being nice to me. "Do you know that your mommy and I kiss a lot?

"Yeah, I see y'all kissing all the time"

"Can you kiss me like your mommy kisses me? Your mommy kisses me on the lips. Can you kiss me on the lips like your mommy does?" You know like this. He moves in slowly to kiss me. He smelled like smoke, but I kissed him back nevertheless. "I like the way you kiss. Your mommy kisses me here too, as he points to his cheek. So I kiss. "She kisses me here too, pointing to the other cheek." So I kiss. "She also kisses me in a very special place. Would you like to kiss me in this special place too?"

"OK". I'll kiss you in the special place because I'm a good kisser right?"

"You are great kissing and if you kiss me in the special place just like mommy does you will the best kisser". By now he is sitting next to me on the bed. He gets up and stands right in front of me. At this moment I feel really happy to be asked to do something that my mommy would do. I loved my mommy and I know that she would be so proud of me for doing this.

"Now this may seem a little weird at first but I know that you will do a good job once you learn. It even took your mommy a few times before she got it right, so don't worry".

I have to say that no true thought passed through my mind as he zipped down his pants and pulled out his penis so naturally as if he had spent he entire life do just that. Pointing to the top of his penis with a determined gaze, he said "Your mommy kisses me right here. Can you kiss right here. All you have to do is just kiss real soft just like you know how to do". So with hesitation I kiss.

"Wow! He says. you are the by far the best kisser ever. I really liked that kiss. Can you do it for me again?"

Even though I enjoy making him happy and being able

to do things that my mommy was able to do, I have to admit that it didn't smell good at all. I didn't want to kiss it again because of the smell and it kind of tasted salty, like peanuts.

"No, I really don't like the smell".

"Oh but I really like the way you kiss me in the special place. Your mommy would be so proud to know that her baby was a great kisser. Oh please kiss me again".

So I kiss. He just looked at me and patted me on my head.

"You did such a great job", as he moved his hand up and down his penis. "Can you do one more thing for me? I know you will do a really good job at this".

"OK"

"I know you like Popsicles".

"Yeah, I like them a lot!"

"Yeah, as he moves his hands up and down his penis while patting my head. "Well this is my very own Popsicle".

"It doesn't look like a Popsicle?" I said

"Well its different then any Popsicle you have ever had. It taste really good and I want you to put it in your mouth just like you would a Popsicle."

I really liked Popsicles, so I didn't see any harm in trying this new Popsicle.

"Well does my mommy put it in her mouth?"

"Oh yes! She loves to put my Popsicle in her mouth. Your mommy is real good at this special kiss and I just know that you will be great at it too."

"OK. How do I do this"

As he beings to give me full instructions on how to put is Popsicle in my mouth and hold it just right, I have trouble holding the whole thing. I can see that he getting a little upset with me so I tried as hard as I could to do exactly what he told me to do.

"If you don't get this right I will tell your mother that you failed at something that was so easy to do. Are you really trying as hard as you can?"

Tears begin to flow from my eyes because I don't want to him to tell my mommy, so I try harder but I start to gag because he is pushing his Popsicle down my throat. This only made him angrier and he pushed my head.

"Come on girl you can do this. I know one thing if you don't hold this Popsicle in your mouth like I told you too I will tell you mommy. You better hold it and hold it right."

I swear that I'm trying as hard as I can but it's to much and just as I think that I can't stand him pushing my head harder and harder onto his Popsicle, I start to chock on the water that's coming out of it now.

I can't breath. Please stop, I say to myself, please stop. Somehow he must have heard my thoughts because he finally let's goes of my head. I split out that water before I could swallow it all. It was so nasty and gummy and it made my stomach sick. I felt so sick that I throw up the little bit that I had swallowed. I throw up all over my nightgown and the floor.

"What was that?"

"That was you, all you. You did it. You made the water come out of the Popsicle. You did it baby! I knew that you would be so great at this. I am so proud of you and I know that your mommy would be too. But I know that your mommy wouldn't like that you made a mess of yourself, so go and clean up before she gets back".

My mommy had a trouble temper and when ever she get mad I would always get it so I knew that I had to clean up this mess and clean it fast. I quickly changed my clothes and brushed my teeth. I had to get the floor cleaner to clean up vomit from the floor, just looking at it made me want to throw up some more.

"You know baby, you did a wonderful job. You did such a good job that I think even your mommy would be jealous", standing there while I'm cleaning up the mess. Your mommy would be so jealous of the great job you did, if you told her she would be so mad at you. You can't tell her because you don't want her to be mad at you, do you?"

"No"

"And because I love you I won't tell her either" startled by the rattle at the door. It was mommy. What do I do? Do I tell her what a great job I did putting his Popsicle in my mouth. I mean I was so good in fact that I made water come out or do I run the risk of her being jealous of me... I don't know what to do.

"She will hate you for being better then her. You can't tell her", he whispered. Mommy came quickly around the corner,

"What are y'all doing?" She notices me cleaning up the Popsicle water off the floor. What happened? Rising up I was faced with the question. I freeze. I don't know what I should say. You could see the anger in her face as if she would spit fire out of her eyes and light me on fire right where I stood. What do I do? I start to panic.

"Girl you better tell me what happened in here before I break your neck".

I pray to GOD please make something come out of my mouth. I knew she would hit me if I did say something, but what do I say. I was so confused but I knew I had to say something...SAY SOMETHING. "What the hell happened"?

"I...I..."

"What the hell is wrong with you?

I can't speak. My brain has stop communication with my mouth.

"You better speak the hell up", as she raises her hand

in her usual poise to strike, I was scared. I want her to stop shaking me. Please GOD help me the only thing my body could produce after the fatal blow to the chest was delivered by the hands of my protector, were tears. They fell fast, hard and with no cession. With each drop I wondered why she hated me.

"Wait! ---Damn! You don't have to hit the girl. She just got sick that's all. I told her to clean up and to go lie down and that you would be home so. He pulls me close to him to save me from a second punch in the chest. The girl got sick that's all and she was just trying to clean it up. Leave her alone. Damn"!

Frustrated by my silence, she storms into the living room taking this time to remind me that I'm not special and had no right to disrespect who she was.

He looked me in my eyes and said,

"See what I told you would happen if you told your mommy. You have to trust me. If you tell her she will hate you forever and you don't want that, do you?"

I knew that she wouldn't be satisfied until she got an

answer. Back to demand a response without haste she asked;

"What made you get sick in the first place?"

Just then I knew that I could never tell her. She would never understand. I only wanted her to love me. She would be so upset with me and would probable beat me more. I don't want her to be upset with me, even if she hates me. I knew no other way but to love her. So in order to keep what love I did have, I responded;

"Nothing, I just got sick".

Tsunami

Now I know what you're thinking…oh my God, how could this happen. If that was me I would have told and he would be in jail. If that was my daughter I would kill him myself…BASTARD!! Listen when it happened to me I wasn't surprised. To me nothing bad had really happened except that I had lied to my mother…so what. Having to suck his Popsicle was happening often, why should I think that anything was wrong. Each time, I got better at it. The Popsicle was harder and cum came faster. I pleased him every time. It had gotten to the point where he wanted me all the time. No one else had time for me so if that's what I had to do to get attention, that's what I had to do. It never crossed my mind that evil was happening. I was good at it … no… great. I was "special" and had a talent that not even my mother was successful at. I ask myself why did it happen to me and why did he choose me. I ask why GOD cursed me to be "special." Even though I look back on it sometimes, I don't believe that experience is what changed the course of my life.

As I sit here getting ready to graduate high school, go off to college and start to a new life, I sometimes regret not telling my mom about what happened to me. Would she had stopped me or protected me from his Popsicle? I often wonder if I would have told her that perhaps she would have never hated me so much that she couldn't stand to live with me, abandoning me all those years ago. Children from my generation of crack and crack addiction frequently lost their parents. Many of my cousins left orphaned by parents due to addiction. This time it was me who saw my mother drive off into the sunset. Unlike a wonderful western movie it wasn't because the Wild Wild West was tamed and order was restored in town but because I was a ungrateful child or was it because I was a financial burden no longer worth my weight in Gold. Perhaps, maybe... you know... I don't know why she left. Here I am a seventeen year old soon to be high school graduate and I still don't know why seven years ago my mother decided that my life would be better if she was not apart of it. That I was totally equipped to transverse through life unaccompanied. My mother, my very own mother, the vessel with held me for months and birthed me into existence discarded me like a used condom filled with the cum from a diseased infested pedophile.

One day my friends and I walked home talking about what we were going to do over the coming summer. Swimming was our main focus that summer. Going to the pool was one of the few things that we could actually do that was still safe. You know as I walked home that day I remember thinking that I had a really great life. As we walked into the parking lot, I saw my mom's new boyfriend sitting in the parking lot in a pick up truck

"Where you going", I asked?

"Ask your mother".

Now he was only about 18 and my mom was about 10 years older then him. I have always thought that he was stupid but whatever. So with innocence and ignorance of my future, I bid my friends goodbye. I'll see them later and head to the apartment to find my mother moving around and talking to herself like Celie in the Color Purple. You know like when she was thinking of leaving Mister. I noticed that her suitcase was at the door. Perched as if aware of is final destination. I jokingly asked where she was going not really anticipating an answer. Her response was surprising if not shocking. It was the quake in my earth that started the tsunami wave of my future. A shift in my foundation so violent and destructive yet calm and calculated, that it whispered in my ear a soothing lullaby of impending death. Rang softly to my heart as if its intention was to comfort me, a falsehood of security that I would become all to familiar with.

That moment in time is etched in my mind like a stop clock as if the power plug was pulled out on my life. THE WORDS. It was her words that stuck me with such force. As they spilled out of her mouth, they plunged head first into the tranquil waters of my soul and disrupted my life, altering my very existence while leaving only myself as a witness to the tragedy. Life at that time wasn't story book perfect but I'm blessed…right. I'm different…right. I'm special…….right! I had that constant lighthouse to guide me to shore. Were my friends were losing in this game against crack, I'm suppose to win. This only happens to them. This doesn't happen to me. My mommy was there for me and I was going to be just like her. I had goals and dreams. I had no fears of finding a fate like the others. I …was… special.

As she kept explaining to me where she was going and why I wasn't going with her, you could see the waves getting bigger. Swelling and growing closer, I was so mesmerized by what I was hearing that I couldn't react. I couldn't move. I couldn't save myself. I couldn't go through this life on my own. I can't do this. Why are you casting out to sea? Mommy! Please don't leave me. My feet had become cemented. Her words like waves just kept coming, growing closer and closer. I naive to its purpose to take me under, I would be lost, unable to recover from this undertaking.

In the sense of danger, many animals will flee in order to save their lives but I did have the good sense of a dog to save myself, I didn't know how. How was I supposed to break from the stronghold that my heart had placed on my feet? Where was I going to run to? She was my refuge. She was my shelter. She was my protection! The waters of her words finally hit its target and punched into me, knocking me down and folding me over. Churning and turning me over and under. Sweeping me away in the rip tide...I was drowning. The chill of the water revived my shock mind, I scream out the only words my tongue could formulate, MMMOOOOOOMMMMMYYYYYY", voice raised to levels of unheard terror.

The waters quickly drowned out my screams and washed away my tears. I always look back and say at that very moment my auto pilot kicked. My mind realizes that I was unprepared for such a cruel introduction into what was to be known as my future. I was unable to swim and was going to die. Panic! I begged my mommy not to leave me, not to dispose of me, to keep me, to love me. I grabbed her legs and demanded for her to say with me. I blocked the door so she couldn't leave me. I did all I could to make her stay. Her plea to let her go just forced me to take on more water. Unable to fight, my heart unable to protect me; my mind stepped in and took control.

The mind is by far the most powerful part of the body. In order to keep me alive, in order to keep me from drowning, and in order to keep the little girl I was from being destroyed by the struggle of survival facing my future; it did the one thing that would save me --- it shut down. My mind had slipped itself into a self induced coma...numb. Protecting my soul from the harm of the of words delivered by my own mother, my mind encapsulated by what seemed like the same cement that had my feet affixed only moments before. I had no feeling left in my body, a heart that went numb and a soul that went quiet. The eternal flame of me extinguished. Death is upon me this day. With no control, I'm forced to watch myself go a drift into the waves of unwanted and forgotten abyss. Left to ask the infinite question…WHY?

I don't even remember breathing until the middle of 5th grade. The world around me came as images across a movie screen. Things seemed to just happen. My life was sinking deeper and deeper everyday into the darkest places of my heart. Standing motionless in the place last left by the tidal wave that took me under, I'm frozen in despair and depression unable to breathe in life, desensitized to the world around me, unable and unwilling to move until she came back for me. I just wanted her to come back _for_ me. I needed her to come rescue me, to save me. I cried until the tears of my eyes matched that of the waters surrounding my heart. I screamed her name until my cries fell silent in the lonely darkness. The anguish I feel daily deepens and spread like cancer in my bones, planting intricate poisoned roots throughout my system.

5

Underwater

This was the first time I thought about death. I thought of death to be my friend. I wanted to meet death. I wanted to die so bad that thoughts of killing me consumed my every thought. I would think about how I would want to go. I could jump off a building but what if I don't die and end up cripple. I could cut my wrist but what if someone finds me and I have to walk around with marks of destruction. Taking a drug overdose was never an option because I could never see myself taking that much drugs. I would always settle on shooting myself but I could never bring myself to do it. I was too afraid that I would survive and end up with a hole in the side of my face and disfigured for life. I prayed that I would be struck by a car but once again survive and end up a living witness to my own crime. As much as death consumed my thoughts, the return of my mom was more prevalent. After many hours of internal feuding I would settle on the notion that if I died I would never see her again however the desire to die never left my spirit.

After the exodus of my mother, everybody around me somehow took on a different face. No one looked the same and somehow treated me with contempt that was as big as an elephant. I knew that I was unwanted and it was no hiding that truth. As I was passed around from one family member to the next I could see their hatred for me as I was now a burden and no longer the cash cow once adored by all. Unprotected, I often found myself discarded by people who once worshiped at my mothers feet. I was labeled an outcast like my name was OJ. If she was here they would not treat me like this. Every second of everyday, questions would race through my mind. Why did she leave? What did I do? What did I not do? What can I do to bring her back? How can I make her love me? Over and over like a broken record, I couldn't move past that song. Those words would settle upon my armor of protection created by my mind, waiting for the moment to eat away at what was left of me on the inside. With my soul underwater and my mind tossed to the dry waste land, more of me died each day.

I finally landed in the home of my grandma, my father's mother, the mother of a man I don't remember. My grandma was an OK lady if you like your life to be equal to that of a dog on a leash. She would pretty much give me and the other grandkids anything we wanted but always with a catch. She had this very subtle way of making you feel guilty for everything that she might have done for you, as if a cup of water was a privilege. She would say, "Oh let her get an ice cream you know she is just like her mother, unable to get anything for herself". Or "don't you like living here unlike living with your mother that would beat you all the time".

From the outside, she was what many would consider a great Christian woman and church was her stage. We would go to church all day Sundays as well as all though the week. The only channel we watched in the house was the church channel.

My grandma was the typical southern transplant in Yankee country. Having been the granddaughter of a slave and the daughter of a sharecropper, she had that smell of resentment towards anything and anybody that tampered with her image of a good Negro. She had once had that picture perfect life. Married to a perfect man that provided her with the perfect American dream, she had money, power and respect within the community, until it was harpooned by her relentless pursuit to control the world. My grandfather, unwilling to play second fiddle to the likes of a woman, found his worth in the bed of another. After twenty seven years of marriage and five children, he walked out on his family.

A woman she knew, nonetheless, which made the

scandal that much more damaging to her ego. With her imaged tarnished, she perfected the art of playing the victim. A role she would perform and teach to her family brilliantly. She would parlay herself around town as the woman scorned and trashed the other woman. The way she would bad mouth that woman you would have thought that she stole him out of her bed at 2 am...brutal but always very tactful in her destruction.

The afternoon my mother left, she came over to my aunts' house, not to comfort me or to provide love to a little girl who just had her life destroyed but what she gave was something that would forecast our relationship. That afternoon she pounded me with wave after wave of rejection. Every word she spoke further drowned me in my sea of hopelessness. Never once did she offer me a Life Preserver. Never once did she extent her heart to help me...not once.

I never felt welcomed at her house, that's possibly why I did stay there long. Her kids, my aunts, all treated me different as if I was a different person to each of them. The oldest was the only one I liked. I always believed that see was not my grandfather child. She looked nothing like him or any of the rest of the children. He was tall and black; my aunt was short and light skinned. His facial features didn't look nothing like what my aunt was blessed with. I often wondered if that was the answer to the question as to why she was able to get away from drama that surrounds the family. She seems different from all the others; from her attitude to her appearance she was different. She moved away soon after my mom left which only created a bigger since of unwantediness. Proving that anyone I loved was destined to leave me.

Next there was the jealous one. I think she thought that I was somehow taking her spot in the family, like I was that special… please. With her five kids, who could. There was no room for anyone else. She made sure that her kids got priority in everything, whether they deserved it or not. I always felt like I was in competition with her or she may have been with me because she would always try to push her kids to one up me. They had to be better then I was. Who cares! I never really liked her attitude…anyway.

There was the full blown crack head aunt that spent most of the time stealing anything that wasn't nailed to the floor and even then she would find a way to steal it. Her and her boyfriend, the poison that he is, would get high and do what they called "trip out." They would move through the house scratching and smelling everybody, looking out the window always thinking that someone was out to get them. I have giving them so much money I should claim them on my taxes. She had four kids and they all seemed to have been bitten with the venom of their mother, doomed to be self destructive.

Finally the baby...spoiled, ungrateful baby, was away at college and my cousins and I would go visit her for the summer. She was married a wonderful guy. He was so nice to all of us when we would visit. He would tell us all the time that we could do anything that we wanted to do and that if we wanted to be anything all we had to do was go to college and get an education. No matter what you do, he would say, go to school, I love you and kiss us all on the forehead. Just that little gesture was sometimes the only good thing in my life.

I guess I wasn't the greatest person to live with because only after less then a year she kicked me out and forced me to move to Pennsylvania with my father. I didn't want to go because I was afraid that my mother wouldn't know where to find me. I had lost everything when she left. All my toys and clothes were given away. Other family member took all our furniture, so I was left with nothing. Stripped of my identity and tossed in the streets as if I was trash. I felt as worthless as a penny with a hole in it.

That year I spent with my grandma was terrible. Terrible in the since that I really felt unwelcome by everybody. I just couldn't shake loose from that spot in the sand where the waves had taken me under. Locked in a cocoon of pain I was unable to feel light across my face, unable to breath in life, and unable to believe that I was now alone in this world. My life changed forever. Looking back at it now, the sexual things I was asked to do had not nearly the same impact to my heart and soul. Perhaps that's why I find power and worth in my sexual adventures and always find my heart without love.

I would have just been better off had she died and maybe my pain wouldn't feel so bad. Did my grandma try and reach out to me the best way she knew how, perhaps. But she was never able to penetrate through my shell, through my rage, through my anger, through my depression. Perhaps I should have given her the benefit of the doubt given the circumstances that she was put in. She herself was discarded by her husband of twenty-seven years for another woman. Maybe she was in pain and I couldn't help her. Maybe I was extra weight on her when she was already down.

We all develop our own defenses when we're hurt maybe this was her way of fighting back, I don't know. What I do know is that she didn't fix me or my broken heart. None of them did. No aunt, uncle or cousin reached out to be and just loved me. I felt like they all turned their backs on me. Again bringing up the question of what did I do to be rejected and ultimately... unwanted.

TRUST | FAITH | LOVE

For a longtime I was silent...submerged...sequestered...secluded...until finally, I surrendered. Giving up on any idea that I was worth the effort. Nobody wanted me nor did anyone love me. Over and over again this story was told to me through the actions of the people tasked with preserving my life.

Similar to that famous unsinkable ocean liner, my heart too pierced by the iceberg of a mother's sins.

An act committed in virtual silence, bled the chambers of my heart and quickly filling my soul beyond capacity. My dreams, waterlogged, undertaken by waves and sunken; a struggle so quick, so unexpected, so unbelievable. The fate of my dreams scrambling to abandon ship, one by one *INNOCENCE, STRENGTH, JOY, PEACE, VIRTUE, LOYALTY, GOODNESS, KINDNESS, TRUST , FAITH AND LOVE* were prioritized by class and selected by Darwin; Only the strong will survive.

Many of them left to take in life's waters unprotected, defenseless, exposed and isolated. *INNOCENCE*, having left me so many years ago, wrote me a note to inform me of the tragedy that lead to its departure. Stating that the night I had my first Popsicle, she was pushed over broad by lies and pain. *INNOCENCE* told me the story of how they had awakened her in the darkest hours of night and ordered her to leave my ship for I didn't want her.

Finding out that my *INNOCENCE* was actually taken from me was agonizing. The realization of the departure of my *INNOCENCE* started a chain reaction of dreams ready to take a deep dive. *STRENGTH ... JOY ... PEACE,* slid away from me with the harmonious rhythm of my heartbeat. With every passing beat I grew weak in trying to hold out hope that my mother was going to return. The thoughts of being unwanted by my own mother robbed me of my *JOY AND PEACE* of mind. It left me desperately wanting to die... to quit... to end.

VIRTUE AND LOYALTY* slipped into a mindless existence, choosing to be blind then to face the pain. *GOODNESS AND KINDNESS* had each other to cling too as they were tossed in the belly of my ship. *TRUST, FAITH, LOVE*; the richest passengers on board my ship, were ordered to rescue boats. These dreams, held at GOD's highest value, loaded themselves into life preservers and sailed to safety in hopes to one day reunite with me. But I was sure I would never see them again.

Sunlight

Looking back on it, as I sit moments away from traveling from innocent academia to post traumatic education, I haven't recovered. High school simply became a place where I could engage my mind for a few hours. Day after day I died. I still haven't lived. I've just learned to cope. I did have good days along my journey but never did I get home.

The Sunday before my grandmother shipped

me off to live with my father in Pennsylvania I prayed to God to help me. That day we went to church as usual up early so we could attend Sunday-school before church. My grandmother was in charge of bringing breakfast and drinks for the kids but the adults would primarily consume all the food. Old bossy people were the makeup of this church. Most of the kids in the church were from our family. This particular day I was really depressed, I just wanted to stay in bed but my grandma had this saying, "if you live here you're going to church."

This didn't make sense to me because my aunt and her boyfriend stayed in the house as well and they didn't go to church. So like a heard of mindless sheep we shuffled off to boredom dealt to us by the hands of an aging man who had no real God in him.   The Pastor of the church really wasn't all that good. He gave me the creeps personally. The way he would look at you as if he would enjoy a Popsicle taste test from one of his younger members of the church. Just plain creepy. His wife, was so fake she had this air about her that just made you sick every time she would come around. The phony smile and dry laugh never did make me feel welcome.

The usual cast of character showed up every Sunday like a long running Broadway play.

The completely dedicated usher who didn't allow sleeping or candying in the holy sanctuary. She would make it her point to get your attention and correct you by any means necessary. The mother of the church, who was so old she met Jesus for her first date. She sat in the same spot every Sunday and just rocked to the music, and you could always count on her to shout out an amen to help the Pastor. The Deacon, now the deacon was a special contributor to the whole Sunday morning church experience. He provided what many might call sideline entertainment. A cheerleader of some sorts. The opening prayer and song was his thang. Deacon gave us a prayer that was so long you'd thought it was a song and a song so long you thought you were back on the plantation. Oh but to see his wife, The Deaconess, break out in dance during service was definitely the highlight of the whole day.

Like clock work she threw her head back, let out a thunderous hallelujah and took off running. This lady had no need for a gym. Her workout was provided every Sunday by GOD. Up and down the aisle, she went screaming and carrying on to the end of her usual manner. Falling across the lap of some poor unsuspected person, truly the only real reason I came to church.

For me there was no entertainment too good that could free me from the whole of the pressure that I was in. I sat in the pews that day and cried. I didn't want to go to live with my father. I didn't even know this guy. My real cousins, the cousins on my mom's side wouldn't know how to get me if I needed them. I would be alone. I knew my grandmother didn't like me but for her to toss me away like this, really hammer home her distaste. As I sat, I cried and prayed to GOD. I didn't ask for nothing, I just cried to him. I had nothing left expect tears and sadness.

I sunk to the oceans bottom and found myself cemented, unable to move...to breath... to think, of what to do next. I just knew that as much as I wanted to die...I wanted to live with the same passion. I wanted to prove to them all hat I was more than they ever thought I would be, I wanted to love but I didn't know how. I didn't know how to live under these circumstances, how to behave in society like a "normal" person. How was I supposed to live buried under the weight of the sins of others. This shouldn't be my cross to bear. I

I was buried by a death of a matriarch and the struggles of siblings. I was buried by the lust of a monster and the weakness of a mother. I prayed and I cried. I cried and I prayed and as I prayed the room became dark. I remember the silence. No drums. No singing. No shouting, just silence. There were no thoughts in my head, no sounds in the air, just silence. In that peace I could hear the whisper of a familiar voice. Just a voice that wrapped me in love like a down quilt on a icy winter morning. His words to me were soft and enchanting. I closed my eyes and listened…

"Rest…Trust…Love…Hope…Imagine…Dream… Seek…Soar…Live… Rest your spirit in me and trust that I will protect you. Love unconditionally and hope for more. Imagine the future and dream of your tomorrow. Seek truth and you shall soar to live out the greatness that I have promised you."

Breaking away, my shell of protection had become loosen from my fixed location and began to rise up within the water. My feet now free and my eyes open I surged to the waters top and burst through the wall of darkness that had left me cold and empty. I could feel the sun on my face. Warming my heart and tickling my soul. I was alive. The water of her words had not killed me and I had survived the tsunami. But my armor had only broken away at the feet and eyes. My arms and legs remained locked away. I just floated home; home to my mother and back to my life.

GOD had made a promise to me. I now had the one thing in life that no one could deny me... HOPE. I had hope. I had something to dream for. I had something to hold on to. As the room began to get louder with sounds of drums and the choir singing, all I could hear was those small whispers. I'll admit that I didn't understand what was whispered to me that day. I just knew in my heart that I was changed. I had lived through my ordeal and even though I was unable to save myself, I had GOD which meant I had HOPE.

I HAD HOPE

Pennsylvania

Pennsylvania was different. Pennsylvania was open. Pennsylvania was clean. Pennsylvania was far. Pennsylvania wasn't home but Pennsylvania was new and I needed new. As much as I hated leaving New Jersey, I knew I had to and with my blessing from God I was able to start a new.

Now living in Pennsylvania, it was quick to see that I was different. I was in a foreign country. This town was nothing like New Jersey. Allentown, Pennsylvania a town made famous by a Billy Joel song and 2 NFL players, was my new home. All I knew it was cold, it was wet and it was white. I had never seen so many white people in my life they were everywhere. They were like cockroaches in the kitchen with the lights off. They were just everywhere you turned… white people.

Snow Bunnies

Cocaine Connections

White House Interns

Bleached Blonds

To top it off I lived, in an all-white neighborhood.

I stuck out like a sore thumb. Being one of five black kids in my new school, I knew I would be in a different world. Starting 6th grade I made friends quickly. My new best friends Holly and Melissa made my time there bearable. Holly was a stone cold rocker chick and introduced me to the hair band s of the 80's. We would rock out to bands like Poison, Motley Crew and White Snake. WE lived and died by MTV and the weekly rock countdown. I must admit that the music was cool and I liked it. It was just her and her mom. Her mom worked a lot so she would have me over all the time.

Now Melissa, on the other hand, was the wild child that introduced me to drinking games and seven minutes of heaven. She was boy band crazy and back then everything was New Kids on the Block. I mean I had everything you could think of when it came to these heartthrobs. I had the bedsheets, comforter, curtains, and I even had trading cards. I had every cassette they every put out and even the concert VHS. Melissa was my kiss boys under the bleachers kind of friend. She would ask me all the time to sneak out of the house with her to go to parties.

White kids knew how to party, thanks in part to their parents. There were plenty of weekends we had PCAP or Parental Controlled Alcohol Parties. That's a party where the alcohol is supplied by parents. Crazy now that I think about it but it was the best way to party then. At least your parents knew what you were drinking and you were in a safe environment... white people!

I had my first white boy kiss. He boy name Chad he

was 6'1 in the 7th grade and had one tactical. He had gotten cancer when he was younger that they cut it off. I actually never seen it but I guessed it looked weird. I actually didn't really get into sex and things like that until I in the eighth grade. I knew about sex and when I was growing up in NJ we would play games like hide and seek. This game was a little different where I grew up. It always let to the boy finding you and you guys grinding on each other like you knew you were having sex. Just with your clothes on. I had given over a dozen blow jobs but never really had a sexual reaction to it. It was mechanical and lifeless. It never, and mean never, looked or felt like SEX to me. So when I finally found my orgasm I was a bit surprised.

The story is, one day I was looking for some sock in my dad's draw. As I was searching I found what looked like a blank VHS. Being curious I popped in the tape and was shock about what I was seeing. Women kissing and sucking nipples, I was drawn in. I could have stopped the tape and been completely turned off but I wasn't. Then I saw it. She was licking his Popsicle. OMG! SHE WAS SUCKING HIS

POPSICLE! I had never seen it done like this. It looked nasty and wrong. Wait wrong? Yes? Something wrong had happened to me. I began to cry. I didn't know why the tears where just streaming down my face. I was confused and something else…turned on. I mean I felt THE TINGLE.

The slight vibration in my pussy hummed, as I watched her suck his dick. She slurped and swallowed him, using both hands to caress him. I was in awe, as if I was watching one of the great painters paint there final masterpiece. The tears stopped and I watched him enter into one of the women. Slow and strong, I watched. She licked her pussy and I watched. This was my first experience of a threesome and I watched. I listened to the moans they made and the expressions they made. I saw what looked like enjoyment on her face and I wanted that. It seems that my pussy like it as well because my brain said, "Touch yourself." And touch myself I did. I placed my hand down my pants and leaned back on the bed. I was wet down there, a sloppy mess of juices. I touched it gently and it was like electrical currents running through my body I was on fire.

Within seconds I was moaning just like the ladies on the video. Panting and grinding on my two fingers. Although this was my first time, it seems like I was a natural at this, I thrusted my fingers inside of my wetness and pumped. Allowing the warm sensation to build inside of me, I ribbed my breast with my other hand and watch him pound this ladies pussy on film. In and out he stroked and I followed his lead.

Let me paint the picture for you. I was 12; I'm half naked with my legs in the air, lying on my father bed, watching a porn movie about to bust my first nut. And just like that my inside erupted and I was released. I was set free. I was no longer a little girl I could feel the shift deep within me. The pressure of life thus far was oozing out of me. My wet fingers let nothing to chance. The milky white substance stained my father's sheets. I didn't care. I laid back and rested in the utopia of my experience. I was in some euphoric sense of begin and I LOVE IT. I had found my happiness. I had found my escape from the pain in my life. I had discovered a reason to live with this horrible man and this racist town. I had found and would find this solace every time I would touch myself. Having had pain so great, masturbation became my greatest escape.

DAD

It didn't take long to realize that my dad and I wouldn't get along. I didn't even know him nor did I care to. He never wanted me so why should I have anything to do with him now. If I had one word to describe my father it would be loser and if I have one word to describe our relationship back then it would be a disaster. We didn't have much of a good start. I didn't really know that much about him except that he was an asshole, a crackhead and a degenerate.

When I first moved to PA, we lived with his girlfriend, a white lady that had to be twenty years older than him. She was a really nice lady and she and I really got along. I guess that my father was really threatened by this because he would go out of his way to try and find reasons to fight with both of us. She took all the fighting harder than I did because she would get sick all the time. She had some form of epilepsy that was triggered by stress. I would always have a help her with her medications. At least once a week he would have an epileptic seizure from the arguments her and my father would have. Hell, if I was her I would be sick all the damn time just having to look him.

She finally got fed up with all the fighting. It was threating her own life however I don't think that would have stopped her. I think she was just tired of being cheated on and lied to. So my journey began once again. Pack up and leave what is comfortable and familiar for another go at the unknown. My father had to take care of the both of us. When he finally found an apartment, we moved within the same neighborhood so that I wouldn't have to change schools.

He and I never talked about anything. I went to school, came home, I did my homework, cooked dinner, went to my room and repeated the whole process over again the next day. I was more his girlfriend then I was his daughter.

Not soon after we moved into our own place, he started taking me to his narcotics anonymous meetings, trying to let me know that he was working his 12 step program.

He said, "I was big part of his recovery."

"Bullshit, I would say. I didn't want to be here. This is your program not mine. You wanted to be here, don't try and drag me into the soup of shit you've created for yourself."

We would go to these meetings that were in the basement of some church or community center. I would listen to people talk about how they loved to get high and how they messed up their lives.

"Keep coming back, it works if you work it," they would say.

The one thing that would always come up was how they hated the fact that they messed up with their children. I would cry at every meeting. Many times people would come up to me and say I was so lucky to have a father that would show me how he was trying to recover and it was great for me to be there. They all wished that they could have a second chance with their children. At one point I did feel luck. I felt like maybe just maybe I would have a normal life and finally have that love that I was missing in my life. So I gave it a chance. I gave it my all. I guess my all wasn't good enough.

I always think back about the time with my father. I really tried to make life better. I would sit up at night and think about my mother how she didn't want me. She never called or wrote a letter or nothing. Now I have my father and we are really trying to make this relationship work over the next 2 ½ years. I was able to make a few friends at school but many of my friends came from the Al-Anon meetings my father made me go to.

My father's Narcotics Anonymous sponsor suggested to him. I participate in his recovery by going to meetings with other teens that had parents that had drug and alcohol abuse issues. The process was really hard at first. I was forced to finally talk about how I felt about not only my father's addiction but also my mother's abandonment. I was able to start the healing process. I remember that after about a year of meetings I was finally able to forgive my father for all that had happened between us.

10

Fuck you

The years passed, which seems like forever. When I entered into the 8th grade I was riding on cloud nine. I missed my mom but I have started something new that was actually turning out to be pretty good. I was 13, maybe I was hormonal. Maybe I was chemically imbalanced. I didn't know. But my father started to date again and what we had built seemed to fade away just as quickly. I had this crazy notion that he was mine. I mean I was cooking and cleaning.

Working around the house trying to make a home just like a wife should. Why did he need to bring in someone else? Was I not good enough? I know that sound crazy but I want it to be just the two of us.

He would never have any time for me anymore. It hurt. Just when I thought we had something special it was slipping away. I rebelled. I lashed out and much as I could. Questioning everything he would do. "How can he do this to me?" I would ask. He would come home late, which really got me upset. I was now the jaded wife/girlfriend at home. I would cook and he not even eat the food. I swear I tried to be the best daughter that I could be but instead I was trying to be his main companion.

This misplacement of expectation would lead to epic fights. He would yell at me and tell me that I would be just like my mother, a doped up whore who he never loved. I just wanted him to love me. I just wanted someone to love me. What would it take to have someone just love me. Could he love me like he loved those nasty women he will go out with?

We would argue constantly. The last day of 8th grade, we had a graduation/award ceremony that he didn't show up for. I was upset but I didn't want to make too big of a deal. I had become accustom to disappointment.

I came home and try to make a peace offering dinner. I pan fried pork chops and butter and hot sauce with Rice-a-Roni. The dinner to me was really good. I waited until 9 p.m. for him to come home when he didn't call or nothing I got really distraught. By the time he came in at about 10 p.m. I was sitting on the couch as soon as he opened the door.

"Where in the hell have you been?" I screamed

"The fuck do you think you talking to?" He yelled backed

"I'm talking to you." I said with anger

"Fuck you" He said

"Fuck you," I said as I rushed to the kitchen before him. It was no way in hell he was going to eat the food that I have made. That bastard would starve for all I care. I racked that rice right into the trash.

"What are you doing you," he asked

"You know what the fuck I'm doing," I said as I grab the pork chops

"I bought that. Put it down." He reached for me

"Well I made it." As he grabs the pan "Get the fuck off of me."

"You know you're going to make me hurt you." Holding the pan and spitting in my face.

"Hurt me then if you have the balls to do it. I'll wait..." As I waiting I looked him in his eyes and never thought in a million years he could hurt me. I just knew that even if he didn't like me he still had some love for me. I knew he could never hurt me. I mean he had already damaged me mentally and emotionally but to think that he could cause physical harm was unthinkable.

"Just as I thought... nothing. You punk ass son of a bitch. You have always been a fucking punk." In the trash goes to pork chops.

"I told you not to throw that away." He was posed to

strike.

I know that I may have pushed his button but I was hurt. I mean I really tried to make it work because I really started to trust him and really find a place in my heart for him. He disregarded my effort and called me selfish. He screamed at me that I was an ungrateful bitch. The nerve! How can he say these things to me? I was really trying can't he see that. I went to school. I was an honor student. I didn't do drugs or drink like my friends did. I thought that I was being a good daughter. How could he not see this? I love him and he couldn't find it in his heart to love me back. Fuck him.

"Put me down." I demanded

But by now he had his hands around my neck

"You needed to find something to do, as he chocked me harder. You are my worst mistake. Your mother was a curse and you are the seed of the devil. As GOD as my witness I will kill you in this house. The next time I tell you not to do something, you fucking demon child, you better fucking listen.

His words began to fade as the lack of oxygen to my brain began to cause a collapse in my consciousness. I was dying. I was dying by the hand of my own father. I had already died an emotional death by the heart of my mother and now he was sent to finish me off. Please dear GOD I pray you meet me at the gates. I wasn't sure if I would make it to heaven. Unwanted here on earth why would I be wanted in Heaven. As the room grew dark he spoke...

"Your time here is over. You must move on. I will lead you and guide through the next phase of your life. Trust in my hand sweet child. I will never leave you nor forsake you. I am with you in ALL THINGS. I have your heart in my hands now and always. Let go of the anger. Release the pain. Dive into my love and I will heal you."

I open my eyes to the sounds of my father's footsteps as he walked away from me. He was to leave me there. Lifeless and scared, I crawled to my room and said nothing to my father. I cried myself to sleep that night. As I drifted off to sleep I heard that voice again, telling me to trust in it. I didn't have the strength to keep going. I begged GOD to just let me die. Why was he keeping me alive? Why would you take me through this pain? Please dear GOD, take me away. All I could hear was *I love you. Trust me.* But GOD if you love me and I should trust you, why cause me so much sorrow? Why cause me so much Heartache. Silence... I heard nothing. His voice would never repeat itself that night. I grew cold. I could feel the stone walls being erected in my soul and around my heart. I vowed never to get hurt again.

The next morning he came to my room and said that I needed to find something to do because I was going to just lie around the house all summer. I said nothing. Worst thing was that he never said he was sorry. When I heard the door closed and locked behind him I sprang up and started packing my stuff. I was out of here but I have no money. I went into my father's room and started to look for some money to catch the bus back to New Jersey. I found $60. Perfect! I knew it would be enough because of bus ticket was only $28. Yes! When I got to the bus stop I call my grandmother, hoping that she would take me back. Seeing that it was her fault that I was here in the first place.

"Hey Grandma, I said in a high pitch, cute and innocence voice, hoping that she wouldn't detect the coldness. I am coming to visit you for the summer."

"What happened," she asked

I try to play it cool but I told her that I just needed to get away. Unbeknownst to me, my father had already called her looking for me.

"What? I'm on my way back to New Jersey don't tell him you talk to me." As I hung up the phone I knew I would never step foot back in this city, back in his house, back in his life. He was dead to me.

I had an hour to wait for my bus to leave that felt like forever.

"Here you are, he yelled from the Greyhound station doorway."

Now everyone was looking at us.

"I've been looking for you. You know I shouldn't have you put in jail, he threatened.

"Why should I go to jail? You are the one who chock me to sleep, I said. I should have you arrested. Why don't you just let me go. You don't want me here and I don't want to be here."

That was all it took. He turned and walked out but not before saying

"You will never be anything worth keeping."

You could hear the faint gaps of the on lookers. To their disbelief, a man would say this to a child. Watching him walk out, I made a choice to live free. As I rolled through town I cried and swore that I would prove him wrong. He was mistaken about me. I was something worth keeping you disgusting son of a bitch.

FUCK FORGIVENESS

11

Home Sweet Hell

I felt like a Puerto Rican straight off the boat. I've walked into a whole different country. This town has really changed since I was last here. The projects I grew up in were just across the bridge from the bus terminal. I knew I had to stop there first before I go to Grandma's house. I had to reacquaint myself to the city. First stop, Broadway Burger. They served the best French Fries with gravy you had ever tasted. Oh my god, they are so good. I can taste them now. Sitting thinking back on how just four years ago I made the decision to start my young life over.

Eating at Broadway Burger and smelling the streets, was like going to a family reunion. I was home. I saw everybody in the projects that day. Everybody remembers me. I talk to everybody. Everything was the same but everything was different. The projects were small to me. They use to feel so enormous and so overwhelming to defeat. The skating rink that was across the street had been turned into a supermarket. The usually suspects were hanging out at the liquor store, begging for treats.

Stopping at my aunt's house, it felt familiar. I had this eerie sense that I just didn't belong there anymore. My cousins, on my mom side, told me stories our friends who died trying to sell drugs. To me, as I looked around the condemned neighborhood, many of them look like they are already dead. The Walking Dead! Space aged zombies, devoid of all hope for the future. I started to ask myself, what I was thinking coming by here. I must be out of my mind. This place is disgusting, a trappings for disaster. How could I go back to Pennsylvania after what just happened between my father and I. I had to make this work or die trying.

I had to visit all of my friends and just hang out for a while before I finally made it to my grandma's house, my soon to be living nightmare. It seems that the only people that were happy to see me were my cousins that I used to spend summers down south with.

"Well here you are again," she smirked. You can't seem to get it together I see. Know your father called me and told me the story."

I don't care what he told her. I sure it wasn't the truth, For had he told her that he chocked me unconscious, she would have a little more compassion then she is expressing right now.

"He asked if I will take it back. Apparently he doesn't want you back in his house. For fear he might kill you. I guess I can. Just know that I'm not going to put up with no shit," she said with such hatred.

My GOD, what did I do? Why was I being punished for this? He was wrong. But you know what, who cares at this point. With that, she had pretty much set the tone of my life with her. I really didn't care at this point I would rather live in the projects with the crackheads and whores then sit in this house with her. But I made the most of the summer, running streets and living the dream.

Yeah right! Be the oldest grandchild I was asked to do everything and everything I did. I did it just to keep from getting into it with my grandmother. The relentless pressure to measure up to some unwritten expectation was suffocating. Every morning that summer I was working. My grandmother, was the first black-owned flower shop in the city. The business was something that she grew and it made her proud. One of the proudest things in her life, she never left you forget that fact. The story goes that once her husband left her for the women she was working with she took and class at the local community college and open a business upon graduation. In that regard she was fearless and self-assured. She did have qualities that one can admire but they were hidden under the onion layers of hate and evil.

My time there shared two agenda, one to keep her from yelling at me about being lazy. She did this with everybody that didn't sacrifice their lives for her dreams. Two, so that I could have some money, to simply do things for myself. I would clean, help customers, deliver flowers, and pick up lunch. Whatever I was asked and wasn't asked to do, I did. I became the go to person for EVERYTHING.

As the summer was coming to an end my cousin Tonya a recent high school graduate, was making her mark in life by going to college. College was something that was always on my radar, thanks the Cosby Show spin–off a Different World. I worshiped that show. It made me want to desperately have the college life experience. Coupled that with Spike Lee's School Daze movie, I knew I was going to be a "Wanna-Be."

Tonya was going to be on her own. I loved her. She was my hero. She had made it out. I wanted to do everything she did. Go to the same school she went to. She went to the

Technical and Vocational High school. I went to the same Technical and Vocational High school. I wanted to play the same sports she played. I ran cross-country, played basketball and ran track just like she did. I just wanted to be like her. In many ways than one and I actually followed in her footstep. Tonya was my light. She had shown me how to get out of the darkness that was surrounding me.

I called Pennsylvania and got my transcripts and prepare to take the entrance exam to get into the same high school she went to. It was a really easy process. I was so ahead of my peers when it came to education. I mean I was learning Spanish and German in the 7th & 8th grades. The school practically begged me to attend their school. I knew that if I could get into the school I will be able to get from around these damn people and have my own life. I was 13 years old and I was determined to make life better for myself. I only needed them to get what I wanted... & I wanted out. They weren't going to hold me back and I wasn't going to let go and let them.

12

My First Love

I saw him on the first day of school. He was an Adonis; 6'3", 215lbs, pecan and sweet. An athlete with a body that was agile, sleek, strong and sculpted. He had a versatility that carried him both on and off the football field. Accomplished on both offense and defense, he commanded respect from his opponents and teammates. He brought power to the game and redemption to my life.

Two weeks into my freshmen year he sat down next to me on the bus and for two years he and I were inseparable. I found it easy to love him, he was my Prince Charming (Prince Charming was actually Snow White's guy) and I his Cinderella. That did matter. Nothing matter to me but him. He filled the void. He saved my life. I search for him the crowd of our graduating class, hoping to lock eyes with my love. QuaNathan Porter.

Qua, as we called him, was the child of a born-again crackhead mother and an absent father. It was because we shared the same lonely past, we bonded out futures together. Our love transcended conventional understanding. From day one we were one of the same. I sit just moments from walking the stage to receive a piece of paper that says I have accomplished a goal, yet all I could think about was what went wrong with my first love.

****

As my soul drifted in the waters of life; beaten, battered, bruised and forgotten, my fleshed rotting in the heat of sunlight, dying of thirst but surrounded by water, he sat by and rescued me. My cries of help were heard and prayers answered. He pulled me into his boat and gave me love that quenched my dehydration. As he pulled me over he spoke words of light over my life. He affectionately stroked my brow and with every stroke released all my anger, all my sadness, filled my empty vessel with rainbows of love; this love was familiar to me. This was the love that I was destined to have in my life. He had finally found me. I was finally found. He gave me bright hues of reds, purples, yellows, oranges and greens sprinkled in his eyes. He patched my bleeding heart with kisses on my lips.

Everyday his unconditional love protected me from negativity and covered me in hope. His love rejuvenated my spirit giving me passion to breathe, to try, to begin again. I loved him and he loved me. This kind of love we had often read about; Romeo and Juliet, Porgy and Bess, Napoleon and Josephine. Mark-Anthony and Cleopatra King come to mind often when I think about how much my heart belonged to him. Everything that I had become was because of him; I owed him my life and intended to honor my debt. Although we were still lost at sea we were together. We had each other to lean and depend on. We provided each other with the same level of commitment. We we're equal out of faith, out of honor and most of all I was loved.

Waiting desperately to forge our comment forward he agreed to tie his soul to mine. He was to break my seal tonight. My seal, stamped the symbol of my destiny, contain the wisdom of earth. The knowledge held within its walls could solve mysteries and change the world. His destination was just beyond my seal. See this wasn't his first time, for he was experienced in this craft and I was ready. I was thirteen. I wasn't scared. I wanted to make love to him because he had my heart and his heart belong to me. He played Rick James and Tina Marie's Fire and Desires in the background; it was just one of the songs that he played for us.

We started off kissing; he gently kissed all over my body, kissing places untouched by human lips. For the first time since my mother left I felt safe. I felt like no one could hurt me now. I had to show him that I loved him. I returned the gesture that he had just performed on me, together we bounded with intensity. Our connection had forged and would remain unbroken. His entry into my body was opposite of my feeling felt previously, it hurt but in a pain that was so welcoming, so involved, so good. With every stroked he pushed aside the girl and imparted his essence into my world leaving the signs of a woman created.

Here I am, Eve, at thirteen.

13

Dark Clouds

Together we had drifted in his boat to our own private island and landed where only we were the inhabitants. Our place in the world was enchanted. The beautiful sea trees as far as the eyes could see, this was out paradise... it was. We had all the things we needed. Mango and Banana trees lined the shoreline, while Coconut trees provided a drum beat to our lives by dropping and releasing its treasure to use daily.

Fish and fowl fought for the privilege to dine with us. Our nights and days were spent just lying on the beach reliving and replaying our memories. Being in love with him was the ultimate fairy tale. Swept away by the charm and elegance that we had found here, our own island, our own private world; we did not need anything we had each other. Our love is going to see us through.

As we baskets in the rays of GOD's smile, I noticed a small dark cloud coming towards us. This cloud looked just like the same cloud that had followed me when I was lost at sea. He desperately tried to reassure me that our skies were clear brighter than ever.

"There were no clouds in the fall off distance," he comforted me.

Regardless of his efforts, that lingering cloud consumed me. I was fixated on that cloud every moment. I watched it day and night. Refusing to eat full course meals that he had been preparing, lobsters and fish sautéed in hazelnut oil was no match for the paranoia that had set in. I was finally happy, safe and loved. I wasn't going to let this cloud, this reminder of my past to ruin it for me. I begin to see the mango and banana trees becoming bare. How we're we going to survive?

Everything was starting to change. The darkness began to fall all over the island. The coconut trees fell silent. The fish and fowl made other plans, other arrangements to no longer seek our company. As my fears of this cloud, as my fears have my past, as my fears of this love being taken from me grew wild and out of control, it turned my life into dark and gloomy existence. I had to do more to protect us. I had to do more to protect me. I couldn't go back out there, lost at sea. I couldn't go back into the darkness. I couldn't lose him. What would I do if love left me again?

I had to do more. Fatally frustrated I ordered him to chase the clouds away. Out of pure love for me he did as I directed. Even though he saw nothing of the sort, it was all in my head. Nevertheless the fear was real to me. So my handsome love of my life stood on the edge of the beach foolishly for me called out to the sky,

"Go away and leave us alone. Go away! Go away!" He tried his best to chase away my nightmares.

He fought with me to make me see that it was all in my mind. I was haunted by my own insecurities. I was a failure. I was never going to have it all. I was never going to have peace. That cloud reminded me of my past and it was slowing creeping into my future.

"What is that going to do," I panicked. "You have to get top of this cloud. I know I've seen it before. You have to do more. I refuse to have my life dark and again. You have to do more. You have to go out there and grab it by the tail and wrestle it to the ground. This dark cloud must be defeated and if you can do it and I will."

I was drunk with fear. I wasn't making sense to him. But he loved me. I pushed him away. I scolded him for loving me. I was damaged. I wasn't worth his love. How could he love someone that has so much baggage? He refused to leave me and let me go. He grabbed me and he held me down and he reminded me that there was no cloud; he tried to love me but in my mind and around my heart was this void. I realized then he didn't see the darkness grooming around us. He couldn't see. He was drunk with Love and I was drunk with fear. He was blinded by the beauty of what we had but I blinded by the terror of being abandoned and rejected again.

I knew it was there. I knew it was coming to get me.

"No one, nobody, nothing can destroy us, he pleaded. The only thing that can destroy us is us. Please come back. Please don't leave me. Don't walk away from our thing," he beseeched.

"But I had to, I cried. I had to secure our future. I can't get away but there is a cloud and I see it. It's coming to get me. This fear was coming to get me and I had to stop it and if you don't I will. I have to stop it I have to..."

That cloud, fear, loneliness, the sense of rejection and abandonment was calling me like a beacon and I ran towards it. Instead hiding in the bosom of his love I chose to leave behind my precious gem. I left my first love to chase away the cloud. I told him I would be back. I knew my place was back on my island with him. I needed to get back but I was stuck out there I was fighting my fears. I finally figured out that I couldn't defeat this cloud. So I ran. I ran back to him. I ran back to his love.

On my way back I smelled freshly prepared fish and fruit and I was thankful. Although he welcomed me back, to my surprise I saw her. I was replaced. I had broken his heart. I was shocked to find another woman healing his soul after I had caused so much damage. I was a hurt person who hurt someone. I was evil. I was no good just like everyone had said. She was eating my food, filling her belly with my man's love. An in an instant, my island was gone. My comfort was gone. My first love was… gone.

14

28

So yeah I see him. Section 3 fifth row sitting there as fine as ever, Qua! He will always be my first love. And even though I pushed him into the arms of other women, we still remained friends. Our two year relationship was magical but it ended, like all things do. It was hard to see him with other women. But I guess it was hard for him to see me with other men. Our relationship was doomed. For over a year before we broke up I was empty. No matter how much he tried to save me I couldn't save myself. I was lost. I was lost to the streets, I was lost to GOD, and I was lost to the possibility of hope for a future. Valentine's Day 1993, QuaNathan brought me flower, a card and candy. He made love to me and like young teenagers we gave our hearts to each other. Dreamt about are lives together and never thought this would be the final time we would see Mecca for a long time.

That particular night I stayed out late from my grandmother's house and when I return home my fate, my next chapter, my destiny was waiting.

"Mecca, where have you been", she said sitting in the dark.

"Out," I replied shock and annoyed she would even ask me about my whereabouts.

"Who do you think you are," rising from the couch. "You think you can do whatever you want. This is not how I operate my house."

"Operate your house, your house…please," I said "This house hasn't been operated by you in years and if you call his operation you have failed. So many people running in and out of here and when was the last time you saw any of your kids. Whatever! Talking to me about operation of your house, bitch please," I said under my breath.

"Get your shit and get the fuck out," she said in low voice of frustration. "You will not come in my house when you want to. I don't give a fuck. Get your shit and get the FUCK out of my house."

"What," not sure as of what she had said.

"Where have you been? She questioned. It doesn't even matter. Get your shit and get out."

I know when I'm not wanted. She kept yelling and I kept packing. The look in her eyes said it all. Just like that I was out on the streets. I didn't even argue. I wanted out. I felt so unwanted here in the first place. Every day was a consistent reminder of my failures as a human being. Being a 3 sport athlete wasn't enough to please her. Being involved in social and afterschool activities that helped other teens wasn't enough for her. I was even a member of the church youth ministry that sang songs on street corners in the city to drug dealers and that even wasn't enough for her. She questioned everything I did and didn't do. I was never right or even heard. I was tired of being her whipping boy. I was tired and here was my chance to be free from her prison.

Me and my black trash bag of belongings at the age of fourteen, was the sum total of my life. I had gone from something to nothing in under 30 minutes. I raced to the one place I thought I could go, Qua's house. His mother quickly showed me that blood is thicker than water and refused to let me stay even for the night. Bags and all she said that it would go against her Christian beliefs if she let her son's girlfriend stay in her house. I was broken. The one place I thought was mine wasn't. Nobody wanted me. Nobody! I cried to Qua and begged him to ask his mother if I could stay. Nothing was going to change her mind. I thought to myself, what kind of "Christian" are you to turn a child on the streets. At 15 I had no one. I had been doing for myself it seemed since I was 14 but now it was real. I was on my own and had to figure this thing out all by myself. SHIT!!!

With my bags in toe, I mustarded up enough courage

to walk to my aunt's home in the projects. Little did I know that my belongings weren't the only things I packed up that night. My pride and self-worth moved out that night too. Dragging my life in a bag, I dropped down on Aunt Janice's couch. She was the family drunk, the oldest living daughter of my dead grandmother. When I use the word drunk to describe my auntie, I mean it to its fullest magnitude. She drank morning, noon and night. She was piss sloppy, fall down and hurt herself drunk. Aunt Janice still seemed to hold down a full time job in the medical field and take care of her drug addicted siblings. They would steal from her every chance they got. It was pretty sad but how can you feel sorry for such a mean lady.

When she was drunk she would cuss you and call you names. I stay with her was more of a duck and dodge. I would make sure I was only there to sleep. We got along for a while with this technique until she tried to kill me. Came at me with a knife and sliced opened two of my fingers as I tried to defend myself. Another place I can't be, don't belong and not wanted at.

I wandered from place to place, house to house, bed

to bed. My routine was to stay for a long as I was invisible. The moment my presence was noticed, it was time to go. Sometimes my stays were weeks and other times only days before I had to find another place. This consent pick of leave, left me homeless. I really never had a place to call me own. It also left me with tough decisions to make, like where to eat and where I was going to stay. No child should have to make those decisions at that age. But I had to, I choose to do the only thing I knew I was good at I…give head. I was good at sex and I knew it. I had finally figured out that what had been happening to me sexually was wrong. What could I do about it, I was good at it, No I was great and people liked it and it made them like me.

It started with guys I knew. Then it was guys I kinda knew, and then it was guys I just met. All so that I could get dinner or have a place to stay. Some guys would just stay nice things to me and I would agree to meet them. Sometimes it was right where we were. I had to eat. I had to have a safe place to sleep. What was I going to do? Starve? Sleep on the street? No I was going to suck a dick. At the end of that first year on my own I had suck and or fuck or in some demoralizing combination of the two had reach an astonishing number. 28. I had counted as recounted the best I could and the number that I could live with was 28.

28 spirits

28 lies

28 broken dreams

28 remembers of false hope

28 repeat offenders

28 forgotten promises

28 men and boys all ejaculated inside of my mouth, my body and eating away at my soul. I was empty. I knew that I was doomed to die soon. I wanted to die. Why should I live? Simply for the satisfaction of a man, no? For the satisfaction of myself? What self. I was nothing and I didn't see anything of worth in me.

Until I met...

15

KING

Knowing I'd Never Go, he wanted me to fulfill his every desire

Knowing I'd Never Go, he sprinkles my desires with promises of love everlasting

Knowing I Never Go, he filled me with hope of a better me

Knowing I'd Never Go, he wrapped me tender goodness that caressed my soul

Knowing I'd Never Go, he used me to fulfill his every desire

Knowing I'd Never Go, sprinkles my desire to the lies of love everlasting

Knowing I'd Never Go, I empty my heart leaving no trace of me

Knowing I'd Never Go, here at me in self-hatred that destroyed my soul

Knowing I'd Never Go, he left the cage open... ***So I left.***

The day I met him I eagerly demanded his affection. My supple body wrote him a personal greeting to join my party and as a respectful guest he did not come empty handed. In spectacular form only as a king could deliver, he ruled over my heart and demanded my worship. 16 to his 22 I was no equal, no match. He was my teacher and I his faithful apprentice. My devotion for him came quick and hard. I fell in love with him. His skin sun kissed and caramel. His physique strong and tone built of Greek mythology. His best gift to me wasn't his love making, which was stellar and by far the best I've ever had to date, but was his ability to make me feel wanted.

I've always knew that he only wanted me for the sex. I was okay with the booty calls and the late night phone calls because I knew he needed me to please him. I was ok with that. I least I thought I was. He was my cousin Tonya's ex-boyfriend. Yes you heard me right. The one person in the world that I looked up, the one person I idolized. I was fucking her ex. Now granted she broke up with him when she went off to college, got married and had a baby all before the ink was dry on the first year of school. By the time we hooked up he was heartbroken. And I was there to easy his plan. The wonderful part about his desire for me was that he was so gorgeous that he could have anyone he wanted but he wanted me... He wanted me.

That's what kept me around, even after he would run to my cousin time and time again leaving me in the bed sometimes just to run to her aid. He knew I was never going to leave. I wasn't strong enough to let go of the something I had with him. He was my hope, my light and also my destruction. With ever sexual encounter I was left with less and less of my soul. After countless hours of me spreading my legs for him he too finally chose someone else. I was old news, the throw away. The story of my life it seems. But this rejection was different. Him turning me away did something to me. It fueled me to break free from the pain I was in. I mean I really looked him in his face and said.

"Not again."

No longer would I be held under his thumb. I was set to graduate from High School and he wasn't going to break me down any further. Actually there was nothing left of me. I was all cried out, I was all turned out, I was all fucked out... at least so I thought.

To Be Contiued...

ABOUT THE AUTHOR

Nikeema Lee is a PhD candidate, Certified Life and Law of Attraction Coach, author, radio and podcast host on the topics of love, sex, and personal healing. She is also a dynamic inspirational speaker traveling worldwide with her one-woman show, as well as, performing with the Pop-Erotica variety show "The Sweet Spot", further reaching audiences of more than a million people, in over 38 U.S. cities.

Nikeema has been featured on Ebony.com, Playboy Radio as well as YourTango.com, the top leading website on love and intimacy. She is a contributor to the all natural sexual enhancement brand Pink Heffs and is a travel sex expert for Grown, Sexy Crew Lifestyle Company taking her coaching to countries throughout the Caribbean and a YouTube star with over 1.3 million views

"My ultimate goal is to assist people on how they can become mentally, spiritually and emotionally free so they can have a great physical relationship."

www.ingramcontent.com/pod-product-compliance
Lightning Source LLC
Chambersburg PA
CBHW070604180626
46817CB00005B/1984